Be My Valentine, Charlie Brown

Be My Valentine,

Charlie Brown

Charles M. Schulz

SCHOLASTIC BOOK SERVICES

NEW YORK · TORONTO · LONDON · AUCKLAND · SYDNEY

Copyright © 1976 by United Feature Syndicate, Inc. Produced in association with Lee Mendelson-Bill Melendez TV Production and Charles M. Schulz Creative Associates, Warren Lockhart, President. Based upon the Lee Mendelson-Bill Melendez television production "Be My Valentine, Charlie Brown." (© 1975 United Feature Syndicate, Inc.) All rights reserved under International and Pan-American Copyright Conventions. This edition is published by Scholastic Book Services, a division of Scholastic Magazines, Inc., by arrangement with Random House, Inc.

12 11 10 9 8 7 6 5 4   9/7 0 2/8

Printed in the U.S.A.

What are you doing, Charlie Brown?

I'm waiting for valentines.

Oh. Well, good luck.

You'll need it!

You didn't have to say that!

The teacher said my name. Did you hear that? Did you hear how she said my name?

Of course she said your name. She was calling the roll.

But it's more than that. I feel that Miss Othmar really likes me. I have the feeling I'm somebody special.

Yes, ma'am? You want me to pound the erasers? Yes, Miss Othmar. I'd be glad to.

Thrillsville!

This proves how much Miss Othmar likes me. It's a privilege and an honor to be selected to pound erasers.

Gasp!

Gasp!

Cough!

I could die from all this honor.

I think I could spend my whole life here and still never get a valentine.

Valentine? That's it! I'll get Miss Othmar the biggest valentine there is. That'll show her how I feel about her! And I can give it to her at our class valentine party.

Wow! A heart-shaped box of candy!

Oh, hi, Violet. I just bought a valentine for Miss Othmar, my teacher.

It's kind of expensive, isn't it?

The amount of money that you spend on a present should be in direct proportion to the amount of affection you have for that person.

You'd better be careful, Linus. It's not a good idea to fall in love with your teacher.

I didn't say I was in love with her. I merely said I'm very fond of the ground on which she walks!

Well, I have a problem, too. What do you give a man teacher for Valentine's Day?

How about shaving lotion?

Do you have any heart-shaped shaving lotion?

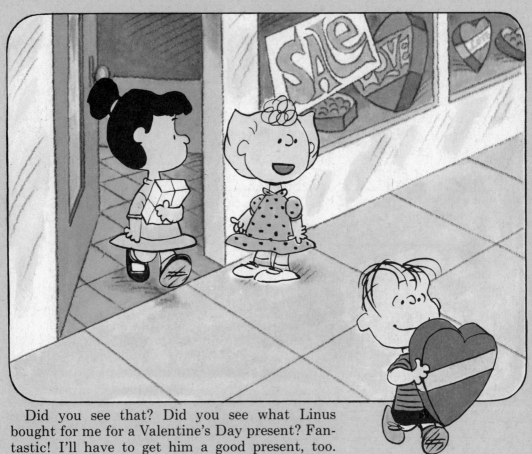

Did you see that? Did you see what Linus bought for me for a Valentine's Day present? Fantastic! I'll have to get him a good present, too. What can a girl get a young man that would be appropriate?

How about a bottle of heart-shaped shaving lotion?

It says here that it is probable the valentine was the first of all greeting cards. Get it, Schroeder? The valentine was *first*. Love comes *first*.

"Originally, Valentine's Day was set aside as a lovers' festival." Oh, Schroeder, isn't that romantic? A lovers' festival.

Sometimes I think you don't realize that you could lose me. Are you sure you want to suffer the tortures of the memory of a lost love? Do you know the tortures of the memory of a lost love?

IT'S AWFUL!

IT WILL HAUNT YOU NIGHT AND DAY! YOU'LL
WAKE UP AT NIGHT SCREAMING! YOU CAN'T EAT!
YOU CAN'T SLEEP! YOU'LL WANT TO SMASH THINGS!

YOU'LL HATE YOURSELF AND THE WORLD AND
EVERYBODY IN IT! OOOOH . . . OOO!!!

Are you sure you want to risk losing me?

Miss Othmar said that if you really like someone,
a homemade valentine is very special.

I can't do it! I just can't do it! I can't fold anything! I can't cut anything! I don't know how to paste!

What's the trouble, Sally?

I'm trying to make Linus a valentine for our class party. You should see the big box of candy that he's bought me! I've got to give him something that is just as good. But I can't even draw a good heart!

Here, let me show you. You get a piece of paper, fold it, and cut out a heart.

Like this.

Try again, Sally.

Good grief!

Well, that's something you can do, too, Sally. Let me try. You take some paper, fold it . . .

Like this. Then you cut diamonds, hearts, moons. Then when you open it, you'll have something nice.

Okay. Everybody put your valentines in the box. Then
we'll have our party and refreshments.

Did you see my name on any of the valentines?

No. I haven't been paying any attention. What's that briefcase for?

Well, in case I get a lot of valentines, I want to have something to carry them in.

I can't get my valentine in the box.
Is it all right if I give it personally?

Miss Othmar, is it okay if Linus
presents his valentine personally?

She says it would be delightful.

She said it would be delightful.

This is going to be better than I expected.

Psst! Linus? I made this specially for you!

Oh, thanks.

What happened?
He forgot to give me
my box of candy!

He's bashful. Ooooh! I'll get him later
with a big smooch.

Okay, okay. If you all sit down, we'll start passing out the valentines.

I wonder if one briefcase will be enough. Maybe I should have brought another one.

Here's one for Sally. And one for Frieda. One for Monte. One for Lucy. And one for Violet. One big one for Tom. One for Peppermint Patty. One for Franklin. And one for Linus. One for Pig-Pen. One for Amie. Another one for Frieda. Here's one for Jill. And here's one . . .

Let's see. Here's another one for Franklin.

Hey, how about one for Charlie Brown?

No, Charlie Brown. When I get one with your name on it, I'll let you know.

Look at that! Charlie Brown still hasn't received a valentine. Did anyone send Charlie Brown a valentine?

Who would waste a valentine on stupid ol' Charlie Brown?

Have a valentine candy, Lucy.

Hey!

Mine says, "Sweet Baby!"

Well, that's it. Happy Valentine's Day, everybody.

Are you sure there isn't a valentine for me?

I'm sure, Charlie Brown. Not one.

Here's my chance. I'd better give
Miss Othmar her Valentine's present.

If you're looking for Miss Othmar,
she's gone. She left a minute ago for
the parking lot.

Here comes Linus with the candy box. This is my big moment! My lover boy approaches with *my* valentine. I think I'll pucker up.

What happened? Where is he? He didn't see me! I had my eyes closed, and he didn't see me. And my box of candy! He still has my box of candy! Where is he going with it?

There goes Linus after Miss Othmar!

I just saw her go by with her boyfriend.

Look at him. He's running to the parking lot! To Miss Othmar's car! With *my* box of candy!!! And there's Miss Othmar with her boyfriend!

Boy, what will he do now?! He's just a crazy mixed-up kid!

I spent all my money. I made a fool of myself.

This one is for love.

This one is for valentines!

And this one is for ROMANCE!

OW! OOOH-OOH-OW!

Hee! Hee!
Ha! H

Well, another Valentine's Day has come and gone.

I'd give anything if that little red-haired girl had sent me a valentine.

Hey! Maybe she *did* send me one. Maybe she sent me a valentine and it didn't get here till today! Maybe it's in our mailbox right now.

I'm afraid to look. If I look and there's nothing there, I'll be crushed. On the other hand, if she did send me a valentine . . . I've *got* to look.

SMACK!

I *hate* Valentine's Day!

Charlie Brown, we've been feeling awfully guilty about not giving you a valentine this year. So, here, I've erased my name from this one. I'd like you to have it.

Hold on there! What do you think you're doing? Who do you think you are?! Don't you think he has any feelings? You and your friends are the most thoughtless bunch I've ever known! You don't care anything about Charlie Brown. You just hate to feel guilty! And now you have the nerve to come around one day later and offer him a used valentine, just to ease your conscience! Well, let me tell you something. Charlie Brown doesn't need your . . .

Don't listen to him. I'll take it!

I guess I let Schroeder down. But it *was* my first valentine, you know.

I didn't do too well either. Miss Othmar went off with her boyfriend. She never even knew I had a Valentine's gift for her.

Well, maybe it wasn't a total flop for me. At least they were showing a little thought for me, even if it was a used valentine. At least they care a *little* bit about me.

Hey, maybe this is the start of a trend. Maybe this is a whole new trend for ol' Charlie Brown. Maybe this is the start of something big!

Maybe next year I'll get a whole bunch of valentines. Maybe next year I'll need three briefcases instead of two. Maybe next year I'll even . . .

Happy Valentine's Day, Charlie Brown.